WUNAMBI

The Water Snake

Written by May O'Brien
Illustrated by Sue Wyatt

ABORIGINAL
STUDIES PRESS

First published in 1991 by
Aboriginal Studies Press for the
Australian Institute of Aboriginal and Torres Strait Islander Studies
GPO Box 553, Canberra ACT 2601
Second edition 2005, Reprinted 2009, 2021, 2023

National Library of Australia Cataloguing-in-Publication Data:

O'Brien, May.
Wunambi the water snake.

New ed.
For children.
ISBN 0 85575 500 8.

1. Aboriginal Australians — Folklore — Juvenile literature.
I. Wyatt, Sue, 1952– . II. Title.

398.20994

Designed by Rachel Ippoliti, Aboriginal Studies Press
Printed by BlueStar Print Group, Australia

About the author

May L O'Brien, BEM, was born in 1933. She worked for the Western Australian Ministry
of Education for 34 years as a teacher and as a consultant to the Aboriginal Education
Branch and finally superintendent of Aboriginal Education. May's contribution to
education and to Aboriginal education in particular was awarded the British Empire
Medal in 1977. She continues to serve on a number of committees on Aboriginal issues.

About the illustrator

Sue Wyatt was born in Kalgoorlie, Western Australia in 1952. She holds a graphic
design qualification from James Street College of TAFE, Perth, Western Australia.
Sue has been holding successful exhibitions of her paintings and drawings since 1971.
She lives in Perth with her family.

This story is dedicated to those generations of grandmothers who did so much to pass on their traditions and to help us understand. It was told to the children by the old people who gathered together at nights to share and to tell of times past.

This is a story of the time when the earth was young and the land was being created. It tells of a powerful and awesome water snake called Wunambi. The Wongutha people of the Eastern Goldfields area of Western Australia say that this huge creature roamed the earth, and that the great tracks it made became the creeks and rivers we know today. Wunambi is still regarded with great respect by Aboriginal people.

Wunambi, the water snake, groaned as he slithered and zig-zagged across the hot and dusty country. He had travelled a long way and was feeling tired. 'I must not stop now,' he muttered to himself. 'I'll just keep going a little bit longer.'

Soon afterwards, Wunambi stopped. 'I must find water quickly,' he sighed. He looked around. It was very hot and everything was so dry. 'There must be water around here somewhere,' Wunambi said. Slowly, he turned and went on his way. His long, shiny body became heavier and heavier. The trail he was making became deeper and deeper.

1

Wunambi stopped again. He rested for a while in the shade of a small tree. The thought of slithering and sliding under and over more jagged rocks made him shudder. Then, in the distance, he saw a small hill. 'I've got to keep going, no matter what,' mumbled the water snake.

His forked tongue flashed in and out of his dry mouth. His head swayed from side to side in time with the movement of his lurching body. Finally, Wunambi reached the hill. Pushing the stones to each side, he slithered smoothly and quietly upwards. 'I'm here at last,' he sighed.

On the hill, zebra finches were busy scratching at the bottom of a deep, dry rockhole. A falling stone warned them that something or someone was coming. Alarmed, the finches flew out.

When they reached the safety of some nearby trees, they twitched their wings and twittered nervously. 'I wonder what it is?' they asked each other. Silently and fearfully, they watched the strange, wriggling creature make its way towards their rockhole.

5

When Wunambi reached the rockhole, he peered into it. It was dry. He closed his eyes for a second. Again he peered into the rockhole. Still there was no water to quench his thirst. 'Just look at that!' hissed Wunambi. 'I'm tired and I've come all this way, only to find a dry rockhole!'

Little by little, Wunambi made his way to a nearby tree. He rested his head on a large rock then his sad, old eyes scanned the countryside.

Suddenly, his head jerked and rose into the air. 'What's that I can see?' he asked himself. He looked again. 'No, it can't be!' Wunambi thrust his head high over the rock to get a better view. 'Yes, there it is. I can see it quite clearly.' Then, shaking his head, he slithered excitedly down the hill into the gully below.

Some pink and grey galahs in the nearby trees saw Wunambi moving awkwardly towards the creek. Sensing danger, they squawked loudly and became restless. They flew from tree to tree, trying to alert others to keep away. The surprised birds and animals watched anxiously as the swaying creature made its way to the water.

Wunambi's weary body ached with every movement. 'Never mind' he thought, 'I'll be in the water soon.' Upon reaching the creek, Wunambi slid noiselessly in to the water. As he sank, the water cooled his long, hot body. 'Oh, that feels so good,' he sighed. Before very long, Wunambi was sound asleep.

9

While Wunambi slept, Aboriginal families were setting up camp near by. They were looking forward to finding bush food.

The children saw the water in the creek. They shouted to each other, '*Gabigudu warurrala!*' (Let's all run fast to the water!) Then they raced towards it.

Before long, they were jumping and splashing in the creek. Ooh, it was cold! It made them shiver and shake, but it felt so good after their long, hot day.

Yelling and shouting, the children chased each other in and out of the water. They thumped and splashed the water with their hands and feet. Their laughter and chatter floated right through the gully, over the tree tops and high into the air.

The noise frightened the emus and kangaroos. They pounded into the bush and watched safely from a distance. The dingoes joined in too. Barking and howling, they raced up and down beside the creek.

The children didn't realise they were sharing the water with a tired old Wunambi. There was big trouble ahead!

Wunambi stirred. He raised his head and listened. He could hear the noise quite clearly now. 'Oh, no! Not those Aboriginal children! I hope they don't stay long. I'm tired. I want some sleep. I hope they go away soon,' he grumbled.

He wanted to go back to sleep, but it was no good trying. The children weren't going to let Wunambi sleep. They were having such a good time. Anyway, they didn't know that Wunambi was there.

Wunambi listened as the noise became louder and louder. Slowly, he opened one tired eye. What he saw jolted him into opening the other. Four dark legs dangled and moved in the water in front of him.

'They're going to tread on me, if they're not careful,' hissed Wunambi. 'I've had enough. I'll teach them not to disturb me.'

15

Slowly, Wunambi uncurled himself. Silently, he raised his head out of the water. Quickly, he glided towards the dingoes. With one quick snatch, Wunambi took one of the dingoes and held it tightly in his mouth. The dingo yelped and wriggled, but it was no use. Wunambi wouldn't let go.

Slowly, the dingo slid down Wunambi's long, wet, slippery throat. Gulp! Gulp! Gulp! Then it was gone.

One of the children saw the water snake. He shouted to the others. '*Bagala warrbuwa*!' (Get up and hurry out!) '*Nhinngi burlganha gabingga*!' (A giant snake is in the water!) '*Nhurrabanha ngula ngalgu, bagala warrbuwa*!' (It's going to eat you, if you don't get out quickly!)

The children screamed and scrambled out onto the bank. By this time, Wunambi had disappeared under the water. Then everything was quiet and still.

17

When they reached the camp, the children shouted and pointed in the direction of the creek. They said, '*Nhinngi burlganggu gabingga, baba guthu manungu!*' (A big snake came out of the water and took one of the dingoes!) While they were telling their parents about the snake, the wide-eyed children kept looking towards the creek.

One of the mothers said, '*Ngaliba nindigu watharra.*' (We know who that could be.) '*Balhanha Wunambiba.*' (It's Wunambi.) '*Balu gamu nhurrabanha ngalgu.*' (He won't eat you.) '*Nhurraba balhunha ma wathala.*' (You must warn him first.)

Another mother said, '*Nhurraba ma yabu gabingga warni.*' (Always throw a stone into the water.) '*Nhurra balhunha wathanhi Wunambigu, nhurra gabingga nhambulathalgu.*' (In that way, you warn Wunambi that you're going for a swim.) '*Balu nhurranha wandigu.*' (Then he'll leave you alone.) The children never ever went into that creek again.

19

That night, Granny told the children the story of Wunambi. She said, '*Wunambi thuningga barnangga mabithangu.*' (The Wunambi glides along the ground.) '*Balu warn burlganha balharanhi.*' (He is making a big, long trail.) '*Warn birdirringu.*' (Some parts of the trail become very deep.) '*Wunambi dalhburringu.*' (This is because Wunambi is tired.)

'*Balu ma gabi warngudu gudiwandingu.*' (Then he sends the rain to fill the trails.) '*Ngaba nhangabaga warn burlgarringu.*' (These trails become creeks.) '*Wunambilu gabi ngala thudinu, thudinu, warn ngaba burlgarringu, burlgarringu, birdirringu, birdirringu.*' (As Wunambi sends more rain, the creeks become wider and wider and deeper and deeper.)

'*Wunambi ngaba thuningga barnangga jina wandigu. Wunambigu thuni barnangga mara-mara mabithangu, ngaliba nhaguranhi.*' (Wunambi leaves his trails all over the country. We can see his tracks as we travel around.)

21

The water snake is very well-known throughout this country. The Aboriginal people of the Eastern Goldfields of Western Australia call him Wunambi. Other Aboriginal people know him by other names. Many stories are told about him.

Paintings of Wunambi can be found on cave walls and his outline is carved on rocks as well. Some people even carve him on their walking sticks, so that they will remember him.

Even today, Wunambi is remembered as an important part of Aboriginal life. You can't see him, but he's there, reminding Aboriginal people of their culture and the rivers and creeks he made for them.

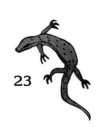

Some sounds in Aboriginal languages and English are the same or very similar, and we have no difficulty speaking and writing them. For example, the letters m, w, l, r, n, y and ng are common. However, some Aboriginal sounds do not occur in English, and we need to use new combinations of letters to express them accurately.

There are three basic vowels in the language spoken at Mount Margaret, which multiply to six because they can be lengthened to form distinct sounds. They are:

- i as in *bina* (ear), corresponding to the sound in 'litre';
- a as in *wathanu* (told), corresponding to the sound in 'father';
- u as in *bulba* (cave), corresponding to the sound in 'put'.

The biggest differences between English and Aboriginal languages are found in the consonants. The language spoken at Mount Margaret has four different 'l' sounds, four 'n' sounds and four 'd' sounds.

One set of sounds in called 'dental' because these sounds are made with the tongue between or touching the teeth. They are indicated by the letter h combined with the consonant, such as 'nh', 'lh and 'th' found in *nhurra* (you) and *wathanu* (told).

The second set of sounds is the 'gum ridge' or 'alveolar' sounds. These are the same as the English sounds 'l', 'n' and 'd'.

The third set is the 'palatal' sounds where the tongue touches or is close to the hard palate of the roof of the mouth. These are the sounds 'ny', 'ly' and 'j' as in the words *jina* (foot) and *nyagu* (to see).

The fourth set is 'retroflex' sounds that are made by turning the tongue towards the back of the mouth. These are the sounds 'rl', 'rd' and 'rn' as in *marlu* (red kangaroo), *gurda* (older brother) and *barna* (ground).

The Mount Margaret language has two 'r' sounds. One is made by trilling the tongue on the gum ridge as in *ngurra* (camp). The other is made with the tongue curled backwards ('retroflex') as in the word *gumuru* (mother's brother).

Special thanks to Dr Toby Metcalfe and to Sadie Canning for their assistance with the language work.

Can you say these Aboriginal words?

Word	Pronunciation	Pronunciation Guide	Meaning
baba	ba-ba	a as in father	dog
bagala	ba-ga-la	a as in father	get up
Balhanha	balh-a-nha	a as in father; lh dental l; nh dental n	that thing or object
balhanu	balh-a-nu	a as in father; lh dental l; u as in put	made
balharanhi	balh-a-ra-nhi	a as in father; lh dental l; nh dental n; i as in i	making
balu	ba-lu	a as in father; u as in put	that person that one
balunha	ba-lu-nha	a as in father; u as in put nh dental n	that one that person that thing that snake
barnangga	bar-nang-ga	a as in father; retroflex rn; ng as in sing	in the ground on the ground
birddirringu	bir-dirr-ing-u	i as in it; retroflex rd; roll rrs; u as in put	deeper and deeper
burlganggu	burl-gang-gu	u as in put; retroflex rl; a as in father; ng as in sing	the big one did
burlganha	burl-ga-nha	u as in put; retroflex rl; a as in father; nh dental n	big one huge one
burlgarringu	burl-garr-ing-u	u as in put; retroflex rl; a as in father; roll rrs; ng as in sing	got bigger got wider got larger
dalhburringu	dalh-burr-ing-u	a as in father; lh dental l u as in put; roll rrs; ng as in sing	got tired or weary
gabi	ga-bi	a as in father i as in it	water
gabigudu	ga-bi-gu-du	a as in father; i as in it; u as in put	to the water

26

Word	Pronunciation	Pronunciation Guide	Meaning
gabingga	ga-bing-ga	a as in father; i as in it; ng as in sing	in the water
gamu	ga-mu	a as in father; u as in put	won't
gudiwandingu	gudi-wan-ding-u	u as in put; i as in it; a as in father; ng as in sing; u as in put	sent
guthu	gu-thu	u as in put	one
jina	ji-na	i as in it; a as in father	feet; tracks
ma	ma	a as in father	went and sent
mabithangu	ma-bith-an-gu	a as in father; i as in it; u as in put	went along; travelled along
manungu	ma-nung-u	a as in father; u as in put; ng as in sing	got; got hold of
mara-mara	ma-ra ma-ra	a as in father	crawling along
ngaba	nga-ba	ng as in sing; a as in father	because of it; therefore
ngala	nga-la	ng as in sing; a as in father	then
ngalgu	ngal-gu	ng as in sing; a as in car; u as in put	eat
ngaliba	nga-li-ba	ng as in sing; i as in it; a as in father	we; us lot; all of us
ngula	ngu-la	ng as in sing; u as in put; a as in father	wont
nhaguranhi	nha-gu-ra-nhi	nh dental n; a as in father; u as in put; i as in it	looking at
nhambulathalgu	nham-bu-la-thal-gu	nh dental n; a as in father; u as in put	going for a swim
nhangabaga	nha-nga-ba-ga	nh dental n; a as in father; ng as in sing	these lot
nhinngi	nhin-ngi	nh dental n; i as in it; ng as in sing	snake or serpent

Word	Pronunciation	Pronunciation Guide	Meaning
nhurra	nhu-rra	nh dental n; u as in put; roll rrs; a as in father	**you**
nhurraba	nhu-rra-ba	nh dental n; u as in put; a as in father	**you lot**
nhurrabanha	nhu-rra-ba-nha	nh dental n; u as in put; roll rrs; a as in father	all of you
nhurranha	nhu-rra-nha	nh dental n; u as in put; roll rrs; a as in father	meaning you
nindigu	nin-di-gu	i as in it; u as in put	know; aware
thudinu	thu-di-nu	u as in put; i as in it	poured
thuni	thu-ni	u as in put; i as in it	stomach or tummy
thuningga	thu-ning-ga	u as in put; a as in father	in the stomach; on the stomach
wandigu	wan-di-gu	a as in father; i as in it; u as in put	leave you alone; will leave alone
warn	wa-rn	a as in father; retroflex rn	creek
warni	wa-rni	a as in father; retroflex rn; i as in it	throw
warngudu	warn-gu-du	a as in father; retroflex rn; u as in put	to the creek
warrbuwa	warr-bu-wa	a as in father; u as in put; roll rrs	hurry up
warurrala	wa-rurr-a-la	a as in father; u as in put; roll rrs	run faster
wathala	wath-a-la	a as in father; u as in put	tell
wathanhi	wa-tha-nhi	a as in father; i as in it; nh dental n	tell or telling

28

Word	Pronunciation	Pronunciation Guide	Meaning
watharra	wa-tha-rra	a as in father; roll rrs	telling or saying
Wunambi	Wu-nam-bi	u as in put; a as in father; i as in it	the name of the mythological water snake
Wunambiba	Wu-nam-bi-ba	u as in put; a as in father; i as in it	it's the mythological water snake
Wunambigu	Wu-nam-bi-gu	a as in father; i as in it; u as in up	belonging to the mythological water snake
Wunambilu	Wu-nam-bi-lu	u as in up; a as in father; i as in it; u as in put	the Wunambi did
yabu	ya-bu	a as in father; u as in put	pebble; rock; stone; hill

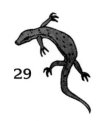